M000076690
HUDSON
PUBLIC LIBRARY
FROM OUR
COLLECTION

WALL OF
WATER

WALL OF WATER

KRISTIN F. JOHNSON

MINNEAPOLIS

Darby Creek
A division of Lerner Publishing Group, Inc.
241 First Avenue North
Minneapolis, MN 55401 USA

For reading levels and more information, look up this title at www.lernerbooks.com.

Front cover: © Nalukai/Paul Topp/Dreamstime.com, (wave); © iStockphoto.com/Marina Mariya (swirl).

Images in this book used with the permission of: © Nalukai/Paul Topp/Dreamstime.com, (wave); © iStockphoto.com/Marina Mariya (swirl).

Main body text set in Janson Text LT Std 12/17.5.
Typeface provided by Adobe Systems.

Library of Congress Cataloging-in-Publication Data

Names: Johnson, Kristin F., 1968- author.
Title: Wall of water / Kristin F. Johnson.
Description: Minneapolis : Darby Creek, [2017] | Series: Day of disaster | Summary: "After a devastating earthquake, a teen and her family are threatened by yet another disaster. A tsunami destroys their house. Their life in paradise is shaken as they try to survive the next blow"— Provided by publisher.
Identifiers: LCCN 2016023632 (print) | LCCN 2016034209 (ebook) | ISBN 9781512427783 (lb : alk. paper) | ISBN 9781512430967 (pb : alk. paper) | ISBN 9781512427868 (eb pdf)
Subjects: | CYAC: Tsunamis—Fiction. | Earthquakes—Fiction. | Survival—Fiction. | Families—Fiction. | Hawaii—Fiction. | Filipino Americans—Fiction. | Racially mixed people—Fiction.
Classification: LCC PZ7.1.J624 Wal 2017 (print) | LCC PZ7.1.J624 (ebook) | DDC [Fic]—dc23

LC record available at https://lccn.loc.gov/2016023632

Manufactured in the United States of America
1-41503-23364-8/3/2016

For my niece, Katy V.

The day of the disaster dawned the same as every other day in Hawaii: perfect. That's what Alexandra's dad had called it when he told her that they would be moving there. Perfect temps, perfect beaches, and perfect weather. A perfect paradise.

But perfect Hawaii didn't have Alex's school, her friends, or her home. Spending her senior year of high school there also meant Alex wouldn't get to graduate with her class. Instead, she would be going to school on Oahu, Hawaii's third-biggest island, with a bunch of strangers. But Alex had no say in the matter, so now here she was with her family in "paradise."

Alex sifted sand between her toes.

"Would you look at that view?" Dad said.

Alex glanced over at him, but said nothing. Her digging toes caught a strand of seaweed left by the tide as it rolled out into the Pacific Ocean. Alex and her family had walked down to the beach to watch the sunrise, their new routine before Mom and Dad headed off to work each day.

"Have a bagel, Alex," her mom said. She spread cream cheese on a bluish roll and walked it over, adding, "You like blueberry, right?"

"Yeah. Thanks." Alex took the bagel and bit into it.

Mom sat down again on her towel, facing the sunrise, and sipped coffee from a mug with *Aloha* written across it in big, cursive letters.

"Can I have some coffee?" Alex asked.

"Nice try," her mom said. "You don't need all that caffeine. You can have some orange juice."

"Yuck." Alex took another generous bite of the bagel.

"Alex!" Drew yelled. "Come over here!"

Her younger brother was running along the beach, playing tag with the tiny waves that crawled inland.

Alex ignored him and pulled the phone out of her back pocket. She texted Simone, her best friend back home in Minnesota, with one hand as she finished the bagel in her other hand. Simone and Alex both had the day off, and Alex hoped they could talk later.

ALEX: Hey!

Waiting. Waiting. Waiting.

SIMONE: Hey.

ALEX: What's up?

Waiting. Waiting. Waiting.

SIMONE: No school! Going 2 movies w/Chase!!! You?

ALEX: Beach. Perfect weather here.

SIMONE: He's here! Gotta go :-)

A pang of jealousy struck Alex as if she had been punched in the stomach. Chase was a guy they both liked. She closed the text window and shoved the phone back into her pocket. She had only been gone from Minnesota for a month and Simone already had a boyfriend. Alex felt like she had hardly met anyone.

Well, that wasn't exactly true. She had made two friends on the island, Sienna and Maia. But they already had a history together, so even though they tried to make Alex feel at home, she was still the new girl. She didn't get any of their inside jokes, and she didn't know any of the places or people they talked about. They just kept saying, *Sorry* and *You'll go there sometime* or *You'll eventually meet so-and-so.*

"Alex!" Mom called. "Get off your phone. You're in Hawaii!"

Alex pushed up off the ground. She dusted the damp sand from her legs and shorts before wandering down to the ocean's edge. The blue-green water was clear enough to see coral, and the sun reflected orange and yellow off the waves farther out. Seagulls swooped and cawed. The air was warm and balmy. It would be another "perfect" day in Hawaii.

"Bet your friends back home are jealous that you're wearing shorts and T-shirts all year," Dad said. "They'll be all bundled up in parkas right now. *Brrrr.*" Dad fake-shivered and sipped his coffee.

The truth was that Alex liked having seasons that changed. It made every few months feel like a new beginning. Mom had put their winter clothes in storage, including Alex's favorite navy blue V-neck sweater, saying, "You won't need that where we're going."

The waves crashed against the shore. Drew raced back from the waves as though the water touching his feet were hot lava.

A sign posted along the beach said, *Preserve Our Natural Landscape. Please Leave All Lava Rocks and Other Natural Elements Where You Find Them.*

Alex picked up a black rock, carefully holding it between her index finger and thumb. She jogged over to her dad, who was smiling at the beautiful colors spread across the sky.

"Look at this." She showed him the lava rock. Tiny craters covered its surface, their edges rough like charcoal against her skin. His smile disappeared.

"Alex, the sign says, 'Leave rocks where you find them.' Besides, it's bad luck. Remember what the guide said?"

"You mean the guy in the 'Hang Loose' tank and flip-flops? Is that the best news source?" Alex asked.

"The locals know what they're talking about," her dad said. "We need to respect their traditions."

"I thought you weren't superstitious, Mr. Science," Alex kidded him.

"Then look it up on your phone," he said. Mom shot him a dirty look, and he added, "When we get home." They had moved because Alex's dad, Michael Reyes, was invited to be a visiting professor in the marine biology department at the University of Hawaii. Mom was a writer for a test scoring company that let her telecommute, which meant she worked from a table in a coffee shop. The Reyes house had always been bookish and a bit *Big Bang Theory* nerdish, so anything the slightest bit "paranormal" usually ended in arguing and Googling for evidence.

"Dad!" Drew said. "I can see the Philippines!" He pointed toward an island in the distance.

"That's not the Philippines, you dork," Alex said, rolling her eyes.

"Alex, don't call your brother names," Mom said.

"Yeah!" Drew stuck his tongue out at Alex.

"The Philippines is a little farther away," Dad said.

"You said it was close enough to visit Grandma, close enough that we might be able to see it," Drew said.

"Okay, I think I exaggerated a little on that one."

"What's that then?" Drew asked.

"Must be Kauai," Dad said. "We'll get there sometime soon."

"What about Grandma?" Drew said.

"Yep. We'll see if we can get over there too. It'd be a shame not to visit when we're this close. She would probably never forgive me if we didn't," Dad said.

Alex turned the lava rock over in her hand. "Why can't I keep this? What's the big deal?"

Her dad folded his arms across his chest. "Better safe than sorry, honey. We're visitors. The beach doesn't belong to us."

The rock felt light, the weight of a quarter or even a dime, though it was more the size of a golf ball.

"Alex, listen to your father," Mom said. She was applying sunscreen to her fair-skinned nose and arms.

Alex stared at the rock in her hand. How could a tiny rock be bad luck?

"*Alex!*"

Alex jumped and dropped the rock. "Fine," she said. Dad shook his head. Mom got up and shook the sand out of her beach towel.

"Are we going to see a real volcano?" Drew asked, distracting Dad.

"Maybe." Dad finally unfolded his arms. "When we get a free day, we could fly over to the Big Island."

"Yay!" Drew said.

"The last great volcanic eruption was in 2008, when Kilauea erupted, and it's still spewing lava into the ocean. When we visit the Big Island, you can see where lava ran onto the highway and stopped right in the middle of the road."

Alex was used to her dad going on about geology and seismology, tectonic plates and volcanic eruptions, so she put her headphones on and turned up that song about breaking up with a first love and leaving home.

Drew got bored with Dad's lecture too and went back to playing tag with the waves. Mom and Dad cuffed their pants and walked through the low tide, carrying their sandals in their hands.

Alex picked up a few other rocks and tossed them into the ocean one by one. She threw the last as far as she could. She scooped up another handful and realized she had picked up the lava rock again. She glanced up. No one was watching her. She slipped the rock into her pocket. It was so light she could barely even feel it was there.

After the sunrise, they walked home. Drew also had the day off from school—it was a teacher's workshop day or something—so Alex and her brother had a whole day to bum around. Alex was meeting Sienna and Maia at the beach later. Maybe she would show them the lava rock.

"Have a good day, kids!" Dad said as he and Mom left for work.

As soon as they were gone, Drew snatched Alex's headphones off the kitchen counter.

"Mind if I borrow these?"

"Ugh. Okay. But don't *wreck* them."

"I won't. *Sheesh.*" Drew rolled his eyes

and nestled the headphones over his ears. He plopped down on the couch, his usual spot, propped his feet up on an armrest, and laced his hands across his chest, partially covering the skateboarder doing a kickflip on his blue T-shirt. Electric guitars and drums blared out from the headphones, probably some heavy metal anthem about rebelling and shaking things up.

"Turn it down," Alex said. "You're going to go deaf."

"What?" Drew said, lifting one side of the speakers away from his head.

"Nothing," Alex said. "Never mind."

Drew didn't seem to care much about fitting in. He had his skateboard, and there was a skateboard park right down the block with tons of kids wheeling around and doing tricks. That was enough for him most days.

Alex pulled out her phone. No new texts. Simone hadn't initiated a conversation in a while. How could her best friend have forgotten about her so quickly? *Chase, that's how.* Oh yeah, they had gone to the movies.

Alex sighed. Maybe she would meet someone here in paradise, but they were already a month into the school year and that hadn't happened yet.

The first weeks at school had been a surprise. For once in her life, Alex's brown skin and dark brown hair blended in, looks-wise, with the other kids because well over half of Hawaii's people were Asian American, Native Hawaiian, or multiracial. But looking like them was totally different than having years of shared memories with them. She almost wished she didn't look so similar. Back home, Alex's blended heritage was unique. Here no one noticed her.

She met Sienna because they were in two advanced placement classes together, English and calculus. They even lived near each other, within walking distance of the beach—which Alex had to admit was pretty cool. Sienna's mom was from Columbia and her dad was from the East Coast, so she got the blended heritage thing. And she was a transplant too: her dad was in the service and had been assigned to Hawaii a few years ago.

Sienna's friend Maia lived on the other side of the beach. Alex felt that she had way more in common with Sienna than Maia did, but Mom had bugged Alex to make more than one friend. Now she could see why. If one person got a boyfriend, you would still have other people to do things with.

Sienna and Maia *were* pretty cool, and she liked hanging out with them. Maybe Hawaii wasn't so bad after all. Maybe it wasn't perfect, but it was getting better.

Her phone buzzed with a text.

SIENNA: See you in a half hour?
ALEX: Yes! See you then!
SIENNA: :-)

Alex straightened up and sent Simone a quick text because she wanted to tell someone she was doing something cool today.

No response.

Right. Date with Chase.

Alex stuffed the phone back in her pocket and grabbed Mom's beach towel off the counter. It still smelled of coffee and Mom's coconut sunblock. On the way to the beach, Alex would knock on Sienna's door, and they would walk the rest of the way together. Maia would meet them by the three palm trees that made a triangle, and they would hang up hammocks—Sienna was bringing an extra for Alex—and chill out all day.

Alex went into the kitchen to grab a water bottle for the road and three small bags of chips. Standing on the tile floor, she felt an odd vibration. Had she left her cell phone on vibrate? Maybe that was Sienna again, asking if Alex could bring something else. Or maybe Simone was finally responding to her text.

Alex pulled the phone out. No one had called. Huh? She could have sworn she felt—

There it was again—more like a rumble. Thunder? She stepped toward the window, still holding the bags of chips.

The floor beneath her moved again. It had to be an earthquake.

"Drew!"

He was half asleep on the couch, headphones blaring and a biography of Tony Hawk open on his chest. Alex ran over and shook his leg. "Drew!"

"Huh?" His eyes fluttered open. "What?"

"It's an earthquake! We have to take shelter! Come on!"

Even as she said it, the tremor shook the ground harder.

Drew rolled off the couch and onto his feet, the headphones wrapped around his neck. The kitchen cabinet doors rattled, and the plates and glasses inside clattered. Then the floor actually moved, and a crack split the middle of the living room ceiling.

"Hide! Quick! Get under something sturdy!" Alex directed.

"Like what?"

"I don't know!"

"The bathroom tub?" Drew asked.

"No. Not *in* something. *Under* something. Quick! Follow me!" Alex grabbed his arm, and they ran into their parents' bedroom.

Drew dove under the bed. "Ow!" He rubbed his head as he scooted underneath.

"Be careful."

Alex couldn't fit under the bed, so she ducked under the next best thing: her mom's desk, up against the wall. Mom had refused to leave it behind, saying that nothing would ever replace that solid oak monster. Alex crawled inside the rectangular cubby and folded up, pulling her knees to her chest. She tucked her head, just like they had done during school tornado drills in Minnesota. She placed her hands behind her neck and interlaced her fingers, protecting her spine. Was that good?

It was a lot different than being in the hallways by the lockers during a drill.

Drew was facedown under the bed. His arms shook. He glanced up at her. Above her, she heard framed photos toppling over on the desktop. One slid off and landed next to Alex: a picture from her parents' wedding. Mom and Dad faced each other, smiling, looking so young. Where were they? Somewhere safe? The ground shook again, and a look of horror crossed Drew's face.

"I forgot Lulu!" he screamed.

"Stay put!" Alex yelled. "There's no time to get your lizard!"

A loud crash came from outside. Drew screamed.

"Cover your head and neck!" Alex shouted.

Instead, Drew grabbed the photo of Mom and Dad, pulled it under the bed, and hugged it.

The rumble reminded Alex of a train, but it felt more like riding the rickety old roller coaster at the amusement park near her old house.

Outside something crashed, sounding like metal and glass shattering. Then suddenly the rumbles stopped. Everything went still.

Alex didn't move at first. She held her breath, afraid another tremor would come, but nothing happened.

"Is it over?" Drew asked.

"Wait," Alex answered. "Stay put."

She took a deep breath and slowly lifted her head. Her hands shook, but she steadied them on the carpet and rolled onto all fours. She peeked out from under the desk and looked up toward the ceiling—and whacked her head on the desk drawer, which had opened halfway during the quake. She slid the drawer closed.

The earthquake couldn't have lasted more than a minute.

When Alex stood up, her legs wobbled.

"Drew," she whispered, "you can come out now."

Drew crawled out from under the bed. His cheeks were red.

"You okay?" she asked, trying to sound brave.

"Yeah." He wiped his eyes. "I'm fine."

"Are you crying?"

"No." Drew sniffled and rubbed his eyes with one hand, the wedding photo clutched tight against his chest in the other. "Is it over?"

"Yeah." Alex glanced over the room, her arms wrapped tight around her rib cage. "I think so."

Drew rubbed his head where he had bumped it on the bed.

"Let me see." Alex pushed aside his longish black hair, which he kept growing out in an effort to look cool, and studied the bump. There was a red mark. "I think you'll be fine. You might have a bruise."

Alex surveyed the room. A jagged crack two feet long broke the yellow-painted wall. A longer crack split the ceiling. Was the foundation crumbling too?

"Come on," she said, almost tiptoeing down the hallway. "I think we should go outside."

Drew ran to his room. "Lulu! Good girl. Good girl. She's fine!" he yelled.

"Glad to hear it," Alex said. Having a lizard in the house gave her the creeps, but so did the geckos that sneaked into the house and climbed the walls.

The rest of the house appeared intact. The bookshelves were bolted to the walls, and the cupboards were designed to withstand tremors. With an active volcano on the Big Island and a history of eruptions and landslides, Hawaii was at high risk for earthquakes. The Big Island was on the fault line. An earthquake was less likely on Oahu, but still possible—obviously.

"Come on." Alex grabbed Drew's arm. "Let's go see if everyone else is okay."

Outside, a few neighbors were already cleaning up damage, but most people were at work on a Monday morning. Telephone poles had fallen down—that must have caused the awful crash. Across the street, a palm tree had fallen right on Mr. Chu's tiny car, smashing the hood. The Chus' yard was full of potted plants and palm trees, and Mrs. Chu often shared the avocados and pineapples she grew with her neighbors. Now fallen coconuts littered the ground like balls in some huge croquet game.

Mr. and Mrs. Chu were retired, so they were home most days, and Alex spotted Mrs. Chu as she righted a plant stand. Next to it, a clay pot with intricate flower carvings lay in pieces. Mrs. Chu's stereo sang with a soloist playing a classical violin piece. She glanced over at them, threw her hands in the air, and then waved.

"Aloha," Mrs. Chu said.

"Aloha," Alex yelled and waved back. The Chus had welcomed Alex and her family right after they had moved in. With her dad's mom in the distant Philippines and her mom's parents far away in Minnesota, it was like having an extra set of grandparents. "Where is Mr. Chu?"

"Napping." Mrs. Chu gestured toward their house. "He probably slept through the whole thing." She made a snoring noise and then laughed. The Chus had lived through several earthquakes, so this was no big deal to them. "How are you enjoying your break from school?"

"Well," Alex said, looking around, "it *was* going fine."

"We're just lucky no one was hurt," Mrs. Chu said.

"Good point!" Alex said. "I'll come over and help you in a minute." She pulled her cell phone out of her back pocket and pointed to it. Mrs. Chu nodded.

Alex wanted to get hold of Mom and Dad. Had the earthquake reached their workplaces? She searched for the bars on her phone. No signal. She had heard cell phones sometimes didn't work in emergencies. She stuffed it back in her pocket.

After helping Mrs. Chu, she could wander down to Sienna's and see if their house had any damage. If it wasn't too bad, they could meet Maia at the beach like they'd planned. They'd share snacks and compare notes about who was dating whom and talk about where they were applying to college. Alex was applying to three schools in Minnesota: Concordia College up north, Mankato State, and the University of Minnesota. Her dad had also suggested the

University of Hawaii.

She and Simone had talked about being roommates in college so they wouldn't get stuck with someone super annoying, but that meant they would have to agree on a school. Simone wanted to go to the University of Minnesota-Duluth, but Alex didn't know if she wanted to move to Duluth. Sienna wanted to get back to the mainland too: she didn't have a major picked, but she was considering schools in California. Last week she'd been really excited about the creative writing program at Mills College.

Alex felt another rumble.

"What is that?" Drew said.

"I'm not sure." A chill ran up the back of Alex's neck. Was another earthquake about to hit? No. This rumble felt different, and the usually calm sound of crashing waves seemed closer than normal.

A look of horror crossed Mrs. Chu's face as she looked past Alex.

Drew pointed behind Alex and shouted, "Look out!"

Alex turned toward the ocean. A wave stretched across it, as wide as she could see and reaching at least two stories high, as high as their house. It was as if an enormous dam had broken—a dam that had been holding in the whole Pacific Ocean—and now a giant wall of water rushed toward them. Alex reached for Drew's hand. But she only grazed his fingertips, and then he was gone.

Alex flailed and tumbled in the water. It was as if she had been thrown into an enormous blender spinning with trees and cars and dirt and glass and plants.

I'm drowning, she thought. *I'm going to die.* She was powerless against the water. She needed air. *Kick your feet*, she told herself. *Kick your feet. But which way is up?* With all the debris swirling around her, she couldn't tell. *Look for the light.* Nothing looked like light she should swim toward. *Where is the light? Am I going to die?*

She kept kicking instinctively but didn't seem to be moving. Suddenly Alex burst through the surface. She gasped for air and then coughed up water she had inhaled. The waves slapped her face, and she treaded water frantically, looking around for her brother.

"Drew! Drew!"

Mrs. Chu's house was under water, except for the roof. *The roof? What happened?* Their whole neighborhood was flooded. Alex didn't see Mrs. Chu or her tiny, smashed car, or the downed telephone poles. She didn't see *any* other people.

Alex's whole body ached. Was she hurt? The water was cold. She kept swimming, hunting for something solid. She couldn't get the taste of saltwater out of her mouth no matter how much saliva she spat out. Murky, muddy water swirled around her. Her arm bumped against a dead fish. It was huge—a tuna? The water covered everything but the treetops. She saw some palm trees floating, torn from their roots. Mr. Chu's car surfaced and crossed the water.

Alex treaded water. "Drew!" she yelled, but she didn't see her brother anywhere. "Drew!"

She shouted again and again, sobbing between each hoarse cry.

What if he died? No. She couldn't think that way. *Where are Mom and Dad?* She wanted her parents. Had the tsunami reached as far as the university campus? Had they been able to get to higher ground in time? And what about Sienna? She lived even closer to the ocean. And Maia? What had happened to them? Alex reached for her back pocket, but her phone was gone, taken by the water. It wouldn't have worked anyway after being submerged for that long. Alex patted down her other pockets in case she had put it into one of those. *No . . . wait.* She felt something, but it wasn't her phone. It was a small lump in her front pocket—the lava rock from that morning.

Alex squinted in the sunlight reflecting off the cloudy water. The waves that had always looked clear were now too silty to see through.

"Mrs. Chu!" Alex screamed, hoping her neighbor had survived. She swam hard, dodging downed branches and jagged chunks of who knows what.

"Mrs. Chu!" Alex saw no one in any direction. "Drew!"

The water was changing. She could feel it moving away, like water draining out of a tub. Alex fought the pull, pumping her arms and legs harder in the opposite direction. The Chus' smashed-in car floated past her. The tide was sucking the water back out, which could mean another wave. "Drew!" Alex screamed. *Where is everybody?*

"Drew!" She treaded water in a circle, searching, tears mixing with the seawater on her cheeks. "Drew!" He was a good swimmer, but this wasn't swimming. This was—

"Alex!" she heard. "Alex!" The sound of splashing came from behind her.

Alex spun around and spotted him, clinging to a downed palm tree near the roof of a house. Whose house? Theirs—or what used to be their house? Was this even still their neighborhood?

"Drew! Wait!" Alex swam toward him, but Drew let go of the palm tree and swam toward her. The current tugged them away from the tree.

"Grab onto something," she called to him. "It's pulling!"

Between them, a couch bobbed in the water like a raft.

"Grab the couch!" Alex yelled.

They raced toward it, bumping debris in the water. Drew got there first and clutched the back. Alex lunged toward it and caught the arm on the opposite end.

"Hold on!" she yelled, tightening her grip on the couch. The water was cold and cloudy, gray from stirred-up mud and sand. The couch was moving fast now, away from the rooftops.

She inched her way around the couch until she reached Drew. "The water is moving out," she said. "The tsunami is sucking the water out. We have to let go. We'll get pulled out with it."

"No," Drew said, clinging to the soaked upholstery. "I can't." He shivered.

"You have to. You'll be washed out to sea." They were already being sucked in that direction. "We'll swim back to that rooftop," she said, pointing at a building sticking up out of the floodwaters.

Drew shivered and gripped the couch till his knuckles turned white. He nodded.

"We can do this together. On three," Alex said, putting her hand on his. "Okay?"

Drew shuddered and said, "Okay."

"One. Two. Three."

They pushed off the couch and swam for the building. Alex flailed and pumped her arms. She turned back to see where Drew was. The coach floated out toward the ocean. Drew was right behind her. They were getting closer to the building, but then the water receded even more. Suddenly, Alex could touch her feet on the ground again. She smiled for a second.

Then the shallow water rippled. Alex and Drew caught each other's eyes. Another massive wave was headed toward them.

"Drew! Go under the water!"

"Alex!" Drew screamed.

"Go under!" Alex repeated. "Dive! Now!"

Drew dove, and Alex took a big gulp of air and dove too as the water slammed into them. The second wave was even more tumultuous than the first. She tried swimming away from the surface this time, hoping to avoid more debris that way, but she found herself caught in a tornado of water, driven helplessly through the wreckage.

Finally, she burst through the surface. She opened her eyes into a flood of light and sucked in air, coughing and gasping. She didn't see Drew. She pushed her long hair off her face and gasped as pain shot down her left arm. She must have injured it in the wave.

Again, the tide tugged her out to sea. She couldn't let the ocean swallow her. Where was Drew? She searched the wreckage that once was paradise—flooded homes, trees torn up by their roots, a small fishing boat stranded on a rooftop, its bow cracked open by a fallen light pole. A man floated by, hanging onto a mattress. Then Drew shot up out of the water several yards away.

Alex swam toward him, paddling with her one good arm and kicking her legs.

"Drew! Over here!" The water pulled at her again. She needed to grab hold of something, anything. "We need to stay on land! Where should we go?"

Drew looked around. "The tree. Let's get to the tree!" He scrambled toward a palm tree that seemed intact, though only ten feet of its branches still showed above the water.

They reached the tree and Drew threw a leg over a thick branch. He struggled to pull himself up and then reached out a hand to Alex. His hand shook. Alex fought her way closer to him and grabbed his arm, but nearly pulled him back in the water.

"Hold on," Alex said. She worked her way down the tree branch to an open section. She swung her legs up and tried to get a grip on the smooth bark, but she kept slipping as the receding water cascaded through the branches. Alex moved down to a thinner part of the branch and finally pulled herself up.

The water level dropped a few feet as she and Drew panted in the branches.

"I want Mom and Dad!" Drew said.

"I know," Alex said. She wished Mom and Dad were there too.

"What if they're dead?" Drew burst into sobs.

Alex reached over to clasp a hand on his shoulder. "You can't think like that. You have to have hope." Even as Alex said this, she hardly believed it herself. "Mom and Dad would want us to be brave. They would expect us to try, so let's at least try," she said. "Or fake it till you make it, as Mom would say."

Drew nodded. His teeth chattered as he repeated, "Fake it till you m-make it."

His face carried cuts and bruises, as if the sea had beaten him up. His skateboarder T-shirt was torn in front, showing a scratch etched into his skin. It was a miracle they had survived the tsunami. Alex thought about Mrs. Chu again, and tears sprang into her eyes. Was there any chance they had survived?

As the water receded, Alex realized they were near the beach. She saw the remains of the Aloha Café: its thatched roof and tiki torches were gone. She looked for the three trees where she and Sienna and Maia hung their hammocks, but she couldn't find them.

"Are we the only ones?" Drew said. "Do you think the water went over the whole island?"

Alex sighed. "I don't know." She looked inland, toward the center of Oahu. Hills rose into mountainous terrain. That had to be the safest place on the island. That's where they would find other survivors. "I do know that we need to get to higher ground. That's where we'll be safe." Alex pointed toward the mountains. "Come on."

6

"Why did we have to move here?" Drew said, climbing over a pile of broken branches.

Alex could hear the sadness in his voice. She didn't want to make him feel worse, but she did have plenty of complaints about moving to Hawaii. Drew was barely holding his tears back, so she kept her criticism of Mom and Dad's decision to herself.

They walked for what seemed like hours across downed branches and deep puddles. A dead horse lay on its side in the water. They had gone horseback riding when they first arrived in Hawaii. The trail guide took them way up the steep hills, but the ranch was on the low ground. The horse probably didn't stand a chance.

An overturned white sailboat with *Mermaiden Voyage* painted in blue on its side sat atop a downed palm tree. Alex stepped over part of a mangled deck chair. The tsunami had ripped the flip-flops off her feet, and her bare feet sloshed through mud.

Squelch. Squelch. Squelch.

Drew stopped and sobbed in place.

"What's wrong?" Alex asked.

"Lulu. She's gone."

"I'm sorry," Alex said. "I know you loved her."

Squelch. Squelch. Squelch.

"Ah!" Alex had stepped on something sharp. She hopped on one foot and held Drew's shoulder to keep her balance as she looked at the bottom of her foot. A sliver of wood stuck at an angle. She bit her lip and tugged at the sliver. "Ow!" she cried as it came free, blood rising in its place. "There. I think I got it out." She set her foot down and kept walking. At first her foot stung, but then the pain eased up.

She had nothing else to protect her feet while she walked. Inches of muddy, opaque water still covered the ground, making it impossible to see where they stepped. If something else cut her feet, she would have a hard time continuing, but they needed to keep going. They had to get to Mom and Dad.

"Ow!" Drew yelled.

"Now what?" Alex asked.

Drew was holding his right foot. "I twisted my ankle."

"Walk it off," she said, offering him her shoulder to lean on.

"Ah. It hurts."

"I know," Alex said. "Just try."

Drew reached for her shoulder but then said, "You're bleeding." He pointed a shaky arm at a bloodstain now growing on the front of her white tank top, seeping down toward the green gecko on the front. Cuts crisscrossed all over her arms and legs, but now the ache in her arm intensified.

Alex twisted around carefully and found a piece of clear glass stuck in her arm. Her hands shook and her heart pounded as she reached for the glass and gripped it. Her breath came in rapid gasps, but she squeezed her eyes shut and yanked the glass out. Sobbing, she tossed it in the water. *This is a nightmare.* She longed to be home in frigid Minnesota, where being bundled up in a sweater and fleece blanket made the coldest days cozy. But she had to keep going. She took Drew's hand and guided him on.

When they had first landed in Hawaii, the warm air was like a blanket. Now, trudging through the muck in water-soaked clothes, that same air felt humid, stifling. Slogging through the water was like walking with weights strapped to her ankles.

She tried to think of something better. Mom and Dad, especially Dad, were always asking Alex what she wanted to be and what she wanted to major in in college. She wasn't all that interested in marine biology, or any other kind of biology, but she didn't want to hurt Dad's feelings by saying that. She loved writing. Mom said if Alex loved what she did for work, then she would never work a day in her life because work wouldn't feel like work. Mom said writers usually majored in English. It was a lot of reading and writing papers. If the tsunami had struck in another six months, Alex wouldn't have even been here. She would have been away at college. But then who would have helped Drew today?

When they first moved in, Mrs. Chu had told her that people might not be very friendly until they had been there at least a year. "People are afraid you won't like living on the island. They're afraid you will move," Mrs. Chu said. "They don't want to get too attached. It makes them sad if you leave."

Alex knew all about leaving—leaving her friends, her school, her old neighborhood. She had cried alone in her room many times over the thought that she would barely have time to adjust to Hawaii before having to start all over again at college. She had figured she could be miserable and lonely for a year, or she could make new friends, knowing she would soon be moving away.

Now, with the tsunami, she didn't even know if her new friends had survived. She only had two. She didn't want to lose them. Drew didn't have many friends either.

"What if Mom and Dad are dead?" Drew said.

He asked what she was trying not to think about, but hearing it was worse: the spoken words made it sound more real. Alex squeezed her eyes shut and balled up her fists. She was worried for Mom and Dad, Sienna and Maia, and Mr. and Mrs. Chu. They could all be dead.

"Come on." She choked down a sob. "We need to keep moving. It's getting dark."

Drew sniffled quietly. Alex knew he was crying, but if she started crying too, she wouldn't be able to stop. Instead she tried to focus on getting them to safety.

Drew's feet slogging through the water behind her sounded like paddles pulling a canoe toward the shore.

"You're doing great," she said.

"Do you think anyone will find us?" Drew asked.

"Of course they will," Alex said, trying to sound as convincing as possible, but she didn't look at him when she said it. "Let's just keep moving."

In truth, Alex wasn't really that optimistic. She just wanted to sound hopeful for Drew, even if it was a lie.

"Look!" Drew shouted.

Alex looked up from the dangerously mucky ground. Drew was scrambling toward a boat jammed between some trees and a rock. The name *Reel Deal* appeared on the stern.

"Why is that fishing boat so far inland?" Alex said, but she knew the answer. The tsunami had carried it this far. *When will we reach the end of the wreckage?*

Drew looked in awe at the boat and ran his hand over the topside. It was the kind of boat their dad had taken them out on once when he went deep-sea fishing.

Seaweed draped over the edges of the boat, and a palm tree rested against the side like a gangplank.

"Hello!" Alex yelled. "Hello!" No one answered.

Drew glanced at Alex and then they raced for the gangplank. Drew limped on his twisted ankle, but he got there before Alex and walked the plank first.

At the top he struck a pirate pose and declared, "*Arrrrrr!*"

"Move it, Captain Hook," Alex said, climbing up the palm tree after him. On deck, she surveyed the boat. Shipwreck was more like it. The decks had been swabbed clean by the tsunami.

"Look for anything we can use," Alex said.

"Aye-aye." Drew saluted her.

"I'm going below to investigate." Alex climbed down a ladder with only five rungs. Then she had a horrible thought: *Where is the owner? What if someone is down here? And what if they are dead? Or alive and furious that we're on their boat?*

"We shouldn't be here," she said aloud, even though Drew couldn't hear her.

She cautiously poked a door below deck. It creaked open.

"Hello?" she said more quietly than before. No one answered. She stepped through the doorway.

Cabinet doors hung open, and fishing gear, plastic dishes, and vinyl cushions were strewn everywhere. Water dripped across the wooden planks in the floor, which was cracked in several places, showing fiberglass beneath.

Alex turned back to the door, but a figure loomed up just as she pushed the door open and she screamed.

It was only Drew.

"You scared me half to death!" she scolded.

"Sorry."

Alex sighed. "Let's see what else is on the boat." She hunted through the rest of the cabinets for anything useful that had survived the tsunami. Life jackets—too late for those. Two beach towels that were soaked through. She laid them out to dry on the boat's narrow foredeck.

She felt awkward picking through someone else's belongings, but she and her brother needed food, even if they had become looters. Alex's stomach growled. What time was it? She hadn't eaten anything since the bagel on the beach this morning. Something crinkled at her feet.

"Score! It's like we really are pirates," Alex said, holding up a bag of potato chips.

"I know you're going to share those," Drew said. He sat down on the floor of the boat and rummaged through the storage space under a bench built into the hull. "I hope we find someone else soon," he added.

"We will," Alex said. She stopped searching and met his eyes, repeating, "We *will*. We have to stay positive. Don't give up."

Their mom had hung a plaque on the wall of the house, right where people could see it on the way out the front door. It said, "Don't forget to be awesome!"

Awesome. That seemed impossible right now. How could she be awesome walking through the wreckage of a tsunami?

She prayed they would find their parents. She would feel better now if they ran into anyone at all.

"Look!" Drew held up a can of flavored water.

"We're splitting that," Alex said, her dry tongue sticking to the roof of her mouth.

"Hello!" someone yelled.

"Who's there?" Alex asked.

"Hello!" the person yelled again.

Alex climbed the ladder and looked around.

"Hello?" Alex yelled. "Is someone there?"

"Where are you?" the voice yelled.

Alex knew that voice. "Sienna? Sienna!"

Drew stopped rummaging as Alex climbed out of the boat and down the tree trunk. Heedless of the wreckage, she ran to Sienna and gave her a huge hug. It was so great to find another person, and someone she knew was even better.

"Mi amiga," Sienna said.

"Mi amiga," Alex repeated. Then she stepped back for a moment. "I'm worried. Where is everybody? Where's Maia?"

"Oh!" Sienna said, "I forgot to tell you. Maia called yesterday and said she couldn't meet us this morning because her parents had decided to spend the break in L.A. They left last night."

"You've got to be kidding me," Alex said.

"Nope."

"Wow. That was lucky for them to have missed this." Alex swept her arm around then shook her head. "My dad said we might visit my grandma in the Philippines this year because we're so close. If only we had gone there now, we wouldn't be here. Crazy."

"I know," Sienna said. Alex led her back to the *Reel Deal*, and they climbed aboard.

"I'm worried about my parents," Alex said.

"Me too. My mom and dad went to work as usual. Nobody had any idea." Sienna shook her head. Then she looked Alex in the eye. "Don't worry. They were on higher ground. They're probably fine. We'll keep looking. My dad's probably out doing rescues with his squad."

Alex blinked back tears and nodded. They stood there a moment.

"What happened to your leg?" Alex asked, looking at the gash on Sienna's left shin. Blood streamed down from the wound.

"I don't know. Something cut me."

"Wait here," Alex said.

Sienna sat down on the deck. Drew was still digging around for more food.

Alex sorted through the mess again, muttering, "Aren't they supposed to always have first aid kits on boats?" More bad luck. The rock in her pocket bounced against her leg.

"It's okay." Sienna waved her off. "It's not bleeding much anymore. I'll be fine."

Alex pulled the bag of potato chips open and thrust the bag toward Sienna. "The first's for you."

Sienna smiled and scooped out a chip, stuffed it into her mouth, and crunched.

"That is the best thing ever!" She handed the bag back to Alex, who took two chips and passed the bag to Drew, who shoved a handful of chips into his mouth at once.

"Eat slowly. We don't know when we'll find food again," Alex said.

Drew returned the bag to Alex.

Alex tapped the can of mineral water with her fingernails in an effort to keep it from spraying. They needed every drop of water they could get. She pulled the top and the can opened with a satisfying fizzle. Alex took a couple of sips and handed the can to Drew.

"Sip. Don't gulp," Alex said.

"I know. Geez."

"Well, follow directions," Alex said.

Drew took two sips.

"When will you stop treating me like a kid?"

"You are a kid."

Drew burped just as he answered Alex, "I'm tweeeeeelve. Ahhhhh." He handed the can to Sienna.

Alex rolled her eyes.

"Typical boy," Sienna said.

"Alex?" Drew said.

"Yeah?"

"What if . . ."

She knew he was going to ask again about what would happen if they never got rescued. What if they died out in the sun? What if . . .?

"Do you think Mom and Dad are okay?"

"I hope so," Alex said. "Grandma lived through a tsunami. Dad said her whole village was underwater. If she survived that, so can we."

"I thought Dad said Grandma's parents died in that tsunami."

Alex sipped the mineral water and stood up without answering him. Sienna sipped from the can and then handed it to Drew.

"Come on," Alex said. "If we stay here, we could die in the heat. We need to keep moving."

Alex wrapped the beach towel around Sienna's shoulders and tossed the other towel to Drew.

"This is the next best thing to sunscreen," Alex said.

"What about you?" Sienna said.

"I'll be fine for a while." She held her arm up to Sienna's for comparison. "I'm way darker than you are."

"True," Sienna said.

A dead barracuda showed its belly to the sun. Alex had seen one at the university's aquarium, where her dad held some of his classes. He had been so excited to work with ocean organisms after teaching for so long in the Midwest. Was the university even there anymore? If the university closed because of the disaster, could they go back to Minnesota? What if Dad was on a boat researching fish when the tsunami hit? Sometimes he went out with the local fishermen to learn more for his lectures. Was Dad even alive?

Alex stepped over a chunk of broken coral. "When we were snorkeling, my dad said you couldn't touch the coral or you would kill it," she said. "Look at it now."

"I know," Sienna said. "It's awful."

The coral should have been underwater. Now it had dried up and died. Stepping on the coral seemed disrespectful, even if it was already dead.

The wreckage stretched as far as Alex could see. The tsunami had clawed its way over the island, devouring everything in its path. In the distance, hills emerged, maybe a mile away.

"What is that shining?" Sienna said.

Something glinted on a mound of sand near a fallen palm tree.

Alex walked closer. "It's lava rock."

Guilt tore at her insides. That couldn't be what really caused all of this destruction, taking that one measly stone from the beach, right? *Never take lava rocks. It's bad luck*, the guide had said. It wasn't as if she took the rock off the island altogether. And these lava rocks were far away from the beach; they were inland, near the hills.

They were bound to see someone else soon, weren't they?

Alex bent down and picked the rock out from under the broken palm branches. She pressed its sharp edges into her palm and turned it over. One side was smooth, the other rough and cracked. Lava was like that: two-sided. She dropped the rock to the ground and stuffed her hands in her pockets. She pulled out the rock she had taken and stared at it. Through the tsunami, that little rock had stayed in her pocket, as if the bad luck of the rock was sticking to her.

She thought of dropping the rock right then and there. Would that put things right? This wasn't where she had picked up the rock.

She needed to get the rock back to the ocean, but they were nowhere near the water right now. Her shoulders dropped, and she stuffed the rock back into her pocket. She would have to keep it until she could return it to the ocean.

Sienna jogged over. "What are you doing?"

"Nothing," Alex said. "Just . . . nothing. I don't want to talk about it."

"Okay." Sienna shrugged.

They kept walking, with Drew trailing behind. After a while, the wreckage lightened up. Eventually they reached an area apparently untouched by the tsunami.

"A road," Drew said. He ran toward the paved highway, and Alex ran after him. Finally. So the tsunami hadn't gone over all of Oahu.

"You know what this means?" Alex said.

"What?"

"Mom and Dad. They might be okay. Maybe the water never reached them." Alex felt a burst of new energy. "Let's walk along the highway. Someone's bound to drive by."

The sunbaked pavement burned the bottoms of Alex's bare feet, so she walked on the sand next to the highway instead. Something rumbled in the distance.

"If that's another earthquake . . ." Drew said.

"*Shhh* . . . listen." Alex stopped walking. The rumble grew louder. "I think it's a car. We'll get them to stop. They have to. Quick! Look presentable."

"What?" Drew said. "Presentable. Is that a joke?"

"Stand up straight," Alex said.

In his torn, filthy clothes, Drew looked like he had been in a fight. Sienna didn't look much better. Alex expected she looked the same.

A pickup truck came around the curve. Alex's mouth was dry and her lips cracked from saltwater and sun. She pushed strands of her hair back behind her ears before she waved to the driver, as if that would make a difference.

The truck slowed to a stop. The driver's door opened, and a man stepped out. His black hair was longer than Alex's, past his shoulders. His white tank top had a surfboard on it, and flip-flops slapped his heels as he walked toward them.

"Aloha," the man said, raising a hand. "Are there just three of you?"

"Yes," Drew said, stepping up.

"I can fit you in the back." He jerked a thumb toward his pickup. "I'm finding survivors and driving them to food and to shelter. They set up a hospital in Honolulu. I'll take you there."

Alex felt tears rise in her eyes. "Thank you," she croaked, and then she coughed.

When they reached the pickup, the man handed them each an ice-cold bottle of water. Alex pressed it up against her forehead and then against the back of her neck. Then Alex, Sienna, and Drew climbed aboard the rusty pickup, which was once maroon but had faded nearly to pink.

Wooden benches ran along the two long sides of the truck's bed. A man and a woman, also in rough shape, were on board already. They slid down the bench to make room.

"Have you seen a little boy? He's three years old," the woman asked before they had even sat down. She held out her phone and showed a photo of a toddler holding a red balloon.

"Does your phone work?" Alex asked.

"We tried calling, but we can't connect. His name is Joseph," the woman said, still holding out the boy's picture.

Dirt smudged the woman's face, and cuts and bruises marred her arms and legs.

Her clothes were torn. The man next to her didn't look over. Were they together? He put an arm around her shoulder and his other hand on her knee, and his gold wedding band shone in the sun.

"We took this at his birthday party." The woman smoothed the picture on the screen with her thumb, as if she was moving Joseph's mussed hair off his face. "We had a juggler. He loves jugglers."

She sounded hopeful. Alex would have to stay hopeful too. *Mom and Dad are alive. We will find them soon.*

Joseph had a smudge of white on his face. Frosting, maybe? His photo disappeared as the screensaver came on.

The woman cradled the phone to her chest. "He likes chocolate cake with white frosting. We told him that not everyone gets to say he spent his third birthday in Hawaii." A sob escaped the woman, and then she inhaled deeply. The man squeezed her shoulder.

"Shhh. It's okay. Shhh," he said.

"I haven't seen him," Alex said. "I'm sorry." She looked down, feeling ashamed, and thought of the lava rock. She tugged at her shirt to make sure it covered her pocket. *How could nature wreak havoc on a little boy like that?*

She wished again that she had never taken the lava rock. She had lost so many other things—her home, her friends, maybe her parents—but that rock stayed with her like a curse she couldn't shake. She had to get it back to the ocean, but now they were driving farther away. The guilt was unbearable. From now on, she would be the best rule follower ever.

"Where are we going?" she asked to no one in particular as the truck jerked forward.

"Aloha Stadium," the woman said. Then she turned off her phone and put it inside her purse. "The Red Cross set up a temporary hospital there. They flew in by helicopter because the main airports are all shut down."

Alex's high school graduation was supposed to be held at Aloha Stadium. Now she might not even be able to graduate.

The man stared down as if studying the ruts in the rusty pickup bed. Worry lines marked his face.

"We're looking for our parents," Drew said. "Michael and Anne Reyes."

"Well," the woman said, "at least you have each other." She put an arm around her husband and kissed his unshaven cheek.

Alex intertwined her hand with Drew's. "We'll find them," Alex said. "We will."

Drew nodded but didn't look her in the eye. Now even Sienna stared down at the ruts in the truck bed.

"And your family," Alex said to Sienna. "We have to stay hopeful."

Alex and Sienna pinky-swore. Alex thought of Mr. and Mrs. Chu again. It was possible they had survived, wasn't it?

Up the road, more people waited to be found. The truck stopped. The tailgate dropped open. People climbed aboard, and the benches filled up. Everyone seemed to be missing someone. The only good thing was that Alex and Drew and Sienna were not alone.

Soon, people pressed shoulder-to-shoulder and knee-to-knee in the truck. But even though she was feeling less alone, Alex just wanted to see her mom and dad.

As they drove up to the stadium, Alex wondered whether it was even safe. The earthquake had shaken the stadium's cement foundation, and cracks like jagged lightning bolts marred the exterior. A mob of people waited at the stadium doors. Were Mom and Dad in that mob? Or already inside? Or somewhere else altogether?

They poured out of the back of the pickup. When Alex stood up, her leg peeled away from the sweaty, hairy leg of the man pressed in next to her.

Inside the open stadium, a Red Cross volunteer handed out sunblock and umbrellas for shade at the stadium's entrance. The University of Hawaii Warriors had played a game last weekend, but now beds covered the yard lines, turning the turf into an enormous hospital ward.

Alex, Sienna, and Drew followed signs to the fifty-yard line, where they were supposed to check in.

"Maybe Mom and Dad are here," Drew said.

"Maybe," Alex said, looking around the huge stadium grounds. So many people milled about that she had already lost track of the couple from the truck, Joseph's parents.

"Your cut," Drew said, limping on his leg. "It's getting worse."

Alex looked at her arm. Blood still oozed from the wound, and it looked hot and swollen. She glanced at Sienna's gashed shin and said, "We all need to get checked out."

An intake worker wearing blue scrubs said, "Over here." She had a clipboard and a form for new arrivals.

"You go first," Alex told Sienna. "We'll find you when you're done."

"Sienna Anderson," Sienna told the intake worker, who escorted her behind a privacy curtain.

A few minutes later, the woman returned. "Name?"

"Alexandra Reyes. And this is my brother, Drew Reyes. Can we stay together?"

The woman nodded and wrote on her form as they went into a curtained space containing a bed on wheels and a tiny table. "Okay. Sit here on the bed, and Jack'll check out that cut."

Alex cradled her arm and climbed up on top of a white sheet. Drew stood by her patiently.

Soon a male nurse called, "Knock knock," and ducked around the curtain, carrying a folding chair. "Let's see what we can do for you."

"She cut her arm," Drew said.

"Did you now?" The nurse sounded Australian. "Let's have a look-see." Alex held her arm out, and the nurse looked it over. "Not just a surface cut, is it now? Right then. Stitches it is. Not to worry. Be right back."

Alex glanced at Drew. He had gotten stitches once above his eye after roughhousing during a kickball game at school. Alex hadn't ever had stitches, but it didn't sound appealing.

The nurse returned with a needle and thread. Stitches meant real stitching.

"This is dissolvable thread, so it will disappear on its own, like a magic trick."

"Are there painkillers? Anything to not feel the needle?"

"No. Sorry. They're preserving that for people with worse wounds than this cut. Right then. We've got to irrigate the wound first. That way we hope it won't get infected."

The nurse cleaned the cut, which stung something fierce, but Alex bit back the pain.

"We need to check to make sure all the glass is out," the nurse said. He held a special light over the cut and examined it. "Looks pretty good. You're lucky."

When the stitching began, Alex turned her head away and tried to think of something else. Watching made her want to vomit. She thought of hanging out with her friends at the beach. She was glad that her friends were okay, but what about all of the other people who had been hurt or killed by the tsunami? That just made her feel sick again. The rock was an uncomfortable lump in her pocket. She focused on the woman across the aisle holding a newborn baby. The woman was alone, except for a doctor and nurse. No husband.

"I will name him Keanu, after his papa." Tears ran down the woman's cheeks.

The nurse squeezed her shoulder. "Keanu it is."

After a few minutes, the nurse stitching Alex's wound said, "All done."

She looked at it. The stitches were in a straight line like stitches on a football, but thinner.

"Who's here with you?" the nurse said. "Is anyone waiting? Your parents?"

Drew piped up, "We're looking for our parents."

The nurse glanced down and then back up again before saying, "Check the boards at the end zone."

"The critical ward?" Drew asked, his lip quivering.

"No. The other end zone. They have boards for people looking for each other. Anyone who has gone through intake is on that list. We update the lists hourly."

"Thank you," Alex said. "Come on," she said to Drew.

"Dad! Mom!" Drew yelled out as they walked, looking all around, as if by some dumb luck they would fall right over Mom and Dad.

In the end zone, five huge bulletin boards were plastered with papers push-pinned to the cork. Each board had a title: *Intake. Critical. Have you seen? Missing. Deceased.*

A girl who looked near Alex's age ran a finger down the names. Her finger stopped. She stared. Disbelief washed over her face. Then the corners of her mouth turned downward and her mouth opened. No sound came out at first. Then the word "No" escaped and turned into a wail.

Alex looked away quickly. She couldn't go there, not yet. They would check that board last. She steered Drew to the Intake board and told him, "You read this column and look for Mom and Dad. I'll start with this one." The *Critical* one. She wasn't sure what to hope for now.

Drew hobbled closer to his list, and they searched side by side. "Look closely at every name. We want to make sure and check every list carefully."

Alex found other people named Reyes listed, but not her parents' names: Michael and Anne.

"Anything?" Alex asked.

"No. Not yet. Wait!" Drew stopped his finger on the last name Chu. "I found Mrs. Chu! I found Mrs. Chu!"

Alex and Drew jumped up and down. Alex felt her cheeks and mouth turn upward. Finally, some happy news. She didn't ask about Mr. Chu. Drew would say if Mr. Chu were also listed.

"That's good. That's great. Keep looking." Privately, Alex wondered if they were now orphans.

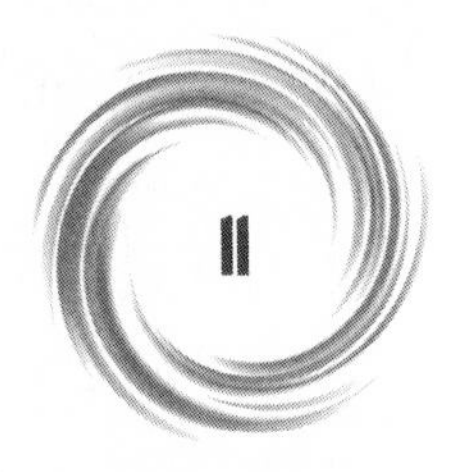

"Alexandra!" The familiar voice came just as Alex started scanning the last page on the Critical list. She turned around, and right there on the Warriors end zone was Mom. Alex and Drew ran over and sandwiched her in a tight hug.

"We thought we would never see you again!" Drew said.

"My family!" Mom said, hugging them tightly.

Alex let go first. "Where's Dad?"

Mom paused. She laid a hand on each of their cheeks. "Your dad's in rough shape. They're prepping him for surgery."

"What?" Alex said. "I thought he would be okay. Wasn't he at the university when the tsunami struck?"

Mom put a hand on Alex's shoulder. "Your dad was on an excursion. The boat capsized, but he was wearing a life jacket. He was lucky."

Again with the luck, Alex thought.

She and Drew told Mom what had happened to them as Mom walked them over to Dad's curtained waiting room in the Critical end zone. Dad grinned and tried to sit up when they arrived, but then winced and stayed in his bed.

"Does it hurt a lot?" Alex asked.

Dad looked down at his shoulder, where the hunk of metal stuck out from his torn white shirt and blazer. "Yeah. It hurts. A lot."

"We thought you had missed the tsunami. What happened?" Alex asked.

Mom brushed a strand of Alex's hair behind her ear. "Dad's team at the university was heading out on the research vessel when the report of the earthquake came in. They tried to make it back, but then the tsunami hit." Mom pointed at Dad's arm.

"It could have been much worse," Dad said. "I wanted to try and pull it out myself, but your mom over there wouldn't let me try."

"Michael, you know if a sliver of metal breaks off, you could have a serious infection. You were just lucky your tetanus shot was up to date."

Alex examined her stitches. Glass didn't cause tetanus. In time the stitches would dissolve and the cut would heal. They were all really lucky.

"Are you going to keep the metal once they take it out?" Drew asked.

Dad laughed. "Ow!" A pained look crossed his face, and he pointed at Drew with a semi-serious grimace. "Don't make me laugh. I'm not sure, Drew. I think I'll just be happy to be rid of it."

"He'll be all right," Mom said.

"How could this have happened?" Alex said.

"Things happen for a reason, honey,"

Dad said. "This happened because there was an earthquake."

"I don't believe that," Alex said. "It was bad luck." She wrung her hands. She needed to talk to someone, but she didn't want her whole family to be mad at her, especially when Dad was about to go into surgery.

Dad's eyes fluttered, and he leaned back on the gurney. The anesthetic was taking effect. Mom bent over, kissed him, and squeezed his hand.

"It's going to be all right," he mumbled. "Kids, wait with your mother while I'm in surgery."

"Just rest, dear." She touched his cheek. "We'll be here when you get out. I love you."

"I love you too," Dad's voice slurred, and he closed his eyes and laid back on the gurney.

A doctor pushed the curtain aside. "We're ready for him now."

Four people came in and rolled Dad out and down the field.

Alex waited with Mom and Drew on hard plastic stadium seats near the surgery area. They each downed a bottle of water and a couple of granola bars flown in from the mainland. Drew found some scrap paper and penciled a picture of their family standing in front of their old house in Minnesota. Alex knew it was the old house because they didn't have pine trees like that in Hawaii.

Drew glanced at Alex.

"I miss home too," she said, meeting his eyes.

Alex felt restless. The surgery seemed to be taking forever. It was all so unreal.

"How long is this going to take?" Alex asked her mom.

"Honey, he's only been in there for a ten minutes."

"I'm going to walk around," Alex said.

"Can I come?" Drew asked.

Alex looked over at Mom. She glanced down at the ground and rubbed her forehead. She was worried.

"No. I want to be alone for a while. You stay here with Mom."

"Awww," Drew whined. Then the corners of his mouth turned downward. "Please can I come with you?" he asked again.

"*No.*" Alex shot him a look to shut up and motioned toward Mom. Drew's shoulders slumped. "I'll be back in a little while." She headed for the perimeter of the stadium.

Near the fifty-yard line, about a dozen kids made pictures with construction paper and pencils. They probably did that to keep them calm. Drawing always seemed to relax Drew. One really little kid caught Alex's eye. He had the curliest brown hair, and when she got closer she saw he was coloring a picture of a red balloon.

"Joseph?" she yelled.

The little boy turned and looked at her.

Alex ran over to him and knelt down. "Are you Joseph?"

He pointed at himself. "I'm free."

She realized he meant to say *I'm three*. He looked just like the boy in the couple's picture. In fact, she was sure it was him.

"Joseph, where are your mommy and daddy?"

He glanced at the sky. "Mommy and Daddy went bye-bye." Tears filled his eyes.

Oh no, Alex thought. *I made him cry*.

A nurse came over. "May I help you?"

"I think I know this little boy's parents. If they're the right people, they're here!"

The nurse's eyes widened. Alex explained about riding in the truck and meeting the couple with the photo of the little boy holding the red balloon. Then she suddenly realized something: "I never got their names." Her shoulders felt heavy. She had told the couple her parents' names, but she didn't ask what their names were.

The nurse said, "Do you think you could recognize them?"

"I'll look for them," Alex said, feeling more determined. "I'll find them! Can you make sure he stays here?"

"Yes, of course." The nurse gestured upward. "Where else would he go?"

Alex ran back to Drew and her mom.

"Drew! Drew! I found Joseph, the boy in the photo. I found him!"

"Wow." Drew smiled. His eyes widened as the enormity of the discovery set in.

"I mean, *wow*." He set down his pencil. "Now can I come with you?"

Before she could answer, someone else called her name. It was Sienna, her leg all bandaged up, accompanied by a uniformed man.

Alex gasped. "I forgot to come find you. I'm sorry. But we found Mom and Dad!"

"It's okay," Sienna said, grinning. "Look who I found!" Her dad waved and introduced himself to everyone. He had to get back to work, but he made sure they had enough water, food, and sunblock before he left.

After Sienna had hugged him one last time, Alex waved her over for a huddle.

"We have a mission," Alex said. "We need to find Joseph's parents."

"Why?" Sienna asked.

"Because they're here at the stadium, and Joseph's here too."

"No way!"

"Yes way," Drew said.

"If we can reunite them, that will be something," Alex said. Inside, she was feeling like that might alleviate some of her guilt over the lava rock.

"Okay," Sienna said. "Where should we start?"

"Well, first, I think one of us needs to get something up on the 'Have you seen?' board, telling his parents that Joseph is here and alive."

"I'm on it!" Drew said. Alex fist-bumped him, and Drew jogged down toward the bulletin boards.

"Okay," Alex continued. "Now we need to search for Joseph's parents. What are your ideas?"

Sienna paused a moment before asking, "Is there a sound system? Maybe we could just have an announcer say their names."

"We never got their names, remember?" Alex said.

"Oh, right," Sienna said.

"But they're here somewhere," Alex said. "We just have to find them."

"Were they injured?" Sienna asked.

"Hmmm. No, I don't think so," Alex said.

"Okay, so we may be able to rule out critical care."

They looked around the rest of the stadium. "It's a lot of ground to cover," Alex said.

"I know," Sienna said. "Hey, let's look at each seating section in order, so we don't duplicate our search. Maybe we'll be lucky."

"Great idea," Alex said. "Let's go!"

Alex and Sienna walked up and down the seating sections, looking for familiar faces. People had scattered over the sections like the few die-hard football fans on a rainy day.

Alex spotted a woman with dark hair sitting two rows up, facing away from them and speaking to someone seated. Was it Joseph's mom?

"Excuse me? Ma'am?" Alex said.

The woman turned around. It wasn't her.

"Oh, sorry," Alex said. "We're looking for someone." The woman was crying. She held a tissue up to her face. "I'm sorry," Alex said again.

The other person rose and hugged the woman as Alex and Sienna hurried away.

"This is impossible," Sienna said.

"We can't give up," Alex said. "We know they came in here."

"But it's like trying to find—"

"A needle in a haystack?" Alex said.

"A pebble in an ocean."

Alex remembered the rock in her pocket. She still needed to return it. Maybe that's why they were having such bad luck in finding Joseph's parents.

"Why are you acting weird?" Sienna said.

"What?"

"You seem off. Is it because you're worried about your dad?"

"Yeah. Yes," Alex lied. "I'm just worried." There, it wasn't a total lie.

They worked their way slowly through the stadium. As they searched sections 103 and 104, Sienna said, "Only half the stadium to go. But my leg hurts. I won't be able to make it too much farther."

Alex sighed. "I know. Let's look through one more section, okay?"

Alex couldn't bear to see one more person

crying or banged up or looking hopeless either, but she felt like she had to go on. People wandered around, dazed and disoriented. Hawaii did not deserve this much bad luck. Paradise had turned into pandemonium.

"There they are!" Sienna said, jarring Alex from her thoughts.

"What?"

"There!" Sienna grabbed Alex's arm, and they hop-shuffled over to a couple sitting about twenty yards away.

"We found Joseph!" Sienna yelled.

The woman looked up at the name *Joseph*. She stared at them for a moment, and then recognition overtook her face. Her hands flew to her cheeks, and her eyes grew wide.

"We found Joseph!" Sienna said again.

"My baby! Where?" the woman said. "Where is he?"

They led the couple to the play area, where Joseph was still drawing pictures with crayons.

"Mommy! Daddy!" he shouted when he caught sight of them. He jumped up from his chair, knocking it over, and ran to his parents, and his mom lifted him up like a quarterback at the Super Bowl.

"We were so worried," Joseph's mom said.

"Thank goodness," his dad said. He glanced over at Alex and Sienna and smiled, mouthing "Thank you." Then he sandwiched his wife and child in a hug.

14

Alex returned to the surgical ward, and Sienna went to rest her leg and wait for her dad's shift to end. Two shadows stood behind the curtains of Alex's Dad's "room." Mom was talking to the doctor, and Dad was lying on the gurney.

"Is he going to be okay?" Mom asked.

"He should recover fine. But he'll need to rest and not overexert himself."

Alex's mom emerged from behind the curtains and draped an arm around Alex's shoulder. "He's going to be just fine," she repeated. "For now, he needs to rest. He's pretty out of it from the surgery."

Alex breathed a sigh of relief. She hoped Dad would be okay. She had a bad feeling, but maybe her luck would change.

Alex felt in her pocket—the rock was still there. She had brought all this havoc and bad luck on her family and Sienna and the islands.

Never take a lava rock. It's bad luck. The guide's words rang in her head. Next time, she would listen to the locals.

She had to return it. That would change her luck.

She wanted to tell her dad. She knew it would make her feel better. She didn't normally keep things from her parents, but she couldn't tell Dad right now because he was still knocked out, and Mom was super stressed already. Alex felt sick.

But she could do something—she could get rid of the rock, once and for all.

"I'll be back," Alex said.

"Where are you going?" Mom called after her, but Alex would explain afterward. She had to get to the ocean.

Alex slipped out a side door and looked around for someone with wheels. She could hitch a ride and get as close to a beach as possible. The stadium was right on the bay, but was that enough? Did she need to return the rock to a natural area like the place she'd found it? Was the beach even there, after the tsunami had clawed at the land?

Alex spotted Sienna, who was sitting in a bent lawn chair with her foot elevated, talking with a cute guy who leaned against a golf cart. He wore a red and white Red Cross T-shirt and looked close to their age.

"Alex, this is Keoni," Sienna said.

"Keo-nee?" Alex said.

"Kee-ony." He smiled as he corrected her pronunciation.

"Sorry. Kee-ony. Is this yours?" Alex pointed at the golf cart.

"Yeah."

"I need you to take me on an errand, if you're willing."

"What do you need?" Keoni asked.

"I need an ocean," Alex said.

"Hmmm." He scrunched up his eyebrows. "Okay. Hop on."

"I'm going with you," Sienna said.

"Okay, you take the front seat," Alex said, "so you can prop up your leg."

"Right." Sienna slipped onto the seat.

Alex climbed onto the back of the cart where golf clubs were normally hauled and hung on to the bars.

Like everything else on the island, the golf cart didn't move fast. Sun sliced under the roof and warmed Alex's arms and legs. Keoni handed her some black emergency sunglasses with a tiny Red Cross on the temple.

She just wanted to get to the water. She couldn't afford to have any more bad luck. Everything she owned had been stolen from her by the tsunami, but that little lava rock would not let go. It clung to her like they belonged together, but she would return it soon.

"You're pretty lucky," Keoni said to them.

Alex laughed. Luck. That was such a matter of opinion. "Why do you say that?" she asked him.

"You survived a tsunami! Do you know how many people die in tsunamis?"

Alex looked down at the floor of the golf cart. She thought of her grandma, who had lost her parents in the tsunami in . . . what had Dad said, 1976? That was before Alex was born. How many people had died in this tsunami? Shame filled her.

"You even found your whole family. That's amazing!"

She glanced at him. "You're right. I should be happier."

Keoni shook his head and kept driving. He told her the news he had heard: the tsunami had crossed much, but not all, of the Hawaiian Islands. There were four or five surges, though the first two had been the worst. The airports were washed over. Planes floated in water, and the most critically hurt patients were being airlifted in helicopters to the mainland.

Alex wondered what Mom and Dad were thinking. Would her family stay in Hawaii and rebuild their lives? Could they even get a flight home? Were they stranded in this disaster until further notice?

After about twenty bumpy minutes of driving, the ocean came into view.

"Here we are," Keoni said. "Waikiki Beach."

Waves crashed into the shoreline, sending water splashing into the air. Keoni drove in as close as he could get, considering the wreckage on the beach, and pulled up in a turnaround about a hundred feet from the water's edge.

"How's this?"

"Good." Alex and Sienna stepped out of the cart and walked toward the ocean. Alex turned for a moment and added, "We'll be right back."

"Take your time." Keoni got out and leaned against the cart, watching the crashing waves.

Seaweed, shells, and dead fish and crabs were strewn about the other litter and wreckage from the tsunami. Alex stepped carefully.

"What are we doing?" Sienna asked.

"I'm making things right," Alex said.

"What are you talking about?"

"I did something, something bad."

"What?"

Alex sighed, exasperated. "I took something, okay?"

"What did you do, take a lava rock?" Sienna laughed.

Alex stared at her for a long moment, stone-faced. "Yeah, I took a lava rock."

Sienna stopped smiling. "Oh," she said.

Alex pulled the rock out of her pocket and held it out to Sienna.

Sienna stared at the stone in Alex's hand, but she didn't touch it.

"Come on," Alex said.

They picked their way down the sand until the cool water lapped at their ankles. They joined hands.

"Please forgive me for stealing the lava rock," Alex said. "I swear I will never take another treasure from your beaches ever again, if you can just make everything all right. And please let my dad be okay."

They squeezed hands. Then Alex gripped the rock, cranked her arm back, and flung the rock as hard as she could over the waves. It landed with a plunk and a tiny splash out in the middle of the water.

A wave, bigger than the others, frothed cold water over Alex's ankles. She felt a sudden wash of gratitude. She had found her family, and her friends were safe. Even though she was covered in bruises and cuts and her cut arm ached, everything would eventually be okay.

Alex led Sienna back to the golf cart. The waves seemed to crash more gently, as if the ocean were relaxing. Or was she just imagining that?

"Feel better?" Keoni asked as Alex settled into the back.

"A little," Alex said. She took a deep breath of fresh ocean air and exhaled. "Are you superstitious?" she asked Keoni.

"Me? I don't know. Maybe. You?"

"Maybe." Alex tightened her grip on the back railing.

Keoni shifted the cart into drive. "Let's get you two *aina hanau*."

Alex gave him a puzzled look.

"Home," he said. "It means home."

"No," she said. "My house is somewhere in the ocean now."

"It's different," he said. "Aina hanau isn't a house—*hale* is the word for the building you live in. Aina hanau is, like, your homeland, where your people are. And it's a lot harder to lose that."

"I think that would be Minnesota," Alex said. "That's where I was born."

"For now, think of it as where your people are. I'll take you back to them."

15

Keoni dropped them off at the stadium, and Alex said, "Thanks for bringing us home."

Keoni just smiled. Alex and Sienna said, "Mahalo!" to thank him for the ride.

"Anytime. Aloha," he said and winked at Sienna before driving away.

"I think he likes you," Alex said.

Sienna giggled and bumped Alex in the shoulder.

More survivors had gathered inside the stadium. The two girls eased through the crowd, careful of Sienna's leg, and arrived just as Mom emerged from the curtained recovery room and waved them in.

Inside, Dad sat with his good arm draped around Drew's shoulder. His other arm was in a sling, and a bulky wrapping covered his wounded shoulder.

"They're saying now that it was a fault-line break in Japan's tectonic plates," Dad was telling Drew.

Fault. No, it was Alex's fault for taking the lava rock.

"And that break rippled into an earthquake on the ocean floor," Dad continued.

Did she dare tell Dad about robbing the beach of its treasure? *I have to tell what I did*, Alex thought. That would be the only way to make the horrible guilt go away. Not telling was making her feel so alone.

"The quake happens on the ocean floor, then creates the huge wave that rolls into shore," Dad continued.

"I have to tell you something," Alex blurted out. She was almost crying.

"What is it, sweetie?" Mom said. "What's wrong?"

Alex didn't deserve them. She shouldn't

have disobeyed the sign and scoffed at the locals' beliefs. How many people had suffered because of what she had done? And Dad had specifically forbidden her from taking the lava rock.

"I took a lava rock," she muttered.

"What?" Mom said. Mom and Dad glanced at each other.

"A lava rock—the ones we're not supposed to take—the ones that cause bad luck, like the guide said."

Recognition washed over Mom's face. "Oh, honey." Mom wrapped her arms around Alex. "You didn't cause this."

Alex stared at the ground.

"Have you been carrying that around all this time?" Mom leaned back to look Alex in the eye.

"Uh-huh," Alex whispered.

Mom pulled Alex in for a tight hug. Alex's shoulders shook as she finally released all the tension she had been carrying.

"That's just an old superstition." Dad waved his good hand in the air. "None of us has that kind of power."

"But tradition here does hold that removing the rocks brings bad luck," Mom said. "Remember the tour guide's stories? People who lost jobs or friends, or who went bankrupt? People might give Alex a hard time for it."

Dad frowned and said, "The people who had bad luck after taking those rocks drew that conclusion, but it was just coincidence."

Alex exhaled, the weight lifting off her shoulders, and then sniffled. "But you said we had to respect what the guide said."

"What? Oh." Dad swatted the air again with his good arm. "I only meant that we needed to respect nature. It's not good for the ecology to remove natural elements from the land or beaches. Maybe removing one lava rock wouldn't make difference, but if *everyone* who visited Hawaii took lava rocks for souvenirs, then it might make a difference."

Alex looked at them. "So what do we do now? We can't go home. Our house is probably gone. Our whole neighborhood is flooded."

Dad thought for a moment. "For now, we'll stay in a temporary shelter and help with the rescue effort. I have a contract with the university for the rest of the school year. Your mom has deadlines. We have obligations. We can't just leave."

Alex had thought they would leave the island immediately. Now, half of her wanted to go back to Minnesota as soon as possible, away from volcanoes and earthquakes and tsunamis, but the other half wanted to stay. She had friends here, Sienna and Maia, and Mrs. Chu. She didn't want to desert them.

Mom added, "Some of the parents were talking while we were sitting in the stadium, and they said the university has already volunteered to let high school classes meet in their classrooms, so you and your classmates can finish out the school year."

"Hey," Dad said, "how about that? It'll be like you get to try college before actually going off to college."

"Hmmm," Alex said.

"We could even carpool together," her dad said.

"Don't push it," Alex said, but then she laughed.

A familiar voice interrupted them. "Hey, Alex! Mr. and Mrs. Reyes!"

Alex turned around. Sienna and both of her parents stood in the end zone, on the *W* in *Warriors*.

Alex ran over and hugged Sienna. "Aloha," she said to Sienna's parents.

"Aloha," they replied.

She turned to Sienna. "I'm so glad you found them both."

Sienna gave a relieved sigh. "Me too. Hey, guess what! We're going to finish the year at the university."

"I heard," Alex said.

"Isn't that lucky?"

Alex looked back at her parents and Drew. They had been lucky—they were all together, alive and well. She thought of Joseph and his parents. They had found each other, but how many other people had been separated from family and friends? Separated from home?

Alex's parents walked over, Drew trailing behind. They were her home. Her family and her friends.

"We're so glad you're all okay," her mom said to Sienna and her family.

Sienna's dad cleared his throat and said, "So, I heard that you have family in the Philippines—maybe somewhere to stay?"

"We do," said Dad. "My mother lives outside Pagadian City."

"Well," Sienna's dad said, "we've had offers from the Philippines to evacuate anyone who's willing, to reduce the strain on resources here. We could get you on the way to your mom's place in a few hours. It will be a few weeks before school starts again."

Mom and Dad exchanged a glance.

"Can you travel right now?" Alex asked her dad.

"The doctor said it was fine, but there would be a wait while they evacuated patients in critical condition. We'll come back when we get the all-clear from the rescue workers and the temporary housing is ready."

"Is that okay with you?" Mom asked Alex.

Alex took a deep breath. She thought of what Mrs. Chu had said, about people leaving. She would find Mrs. Chu before they left and tell her they were coming back.

"Yes," Alex said. "I want to meet Grandma."

"Great!" Dad said. "It will be like going home."

"Aina hanau," Alex said.

"Hyena?" Drew said.

"Aina hanau," Alex repeated. "It means homeland, like going home."

AFTERSHOCK

BACKFIRE

BLACK BLIZZARD

DEEP FREEZE

VORTEX

WALL OF WATER

Would you survive?

About the Author

Kristin F. Johnson lives in Minneapolis, Minnesota, and teaches writing at a local college. She spent two years as a media specialist and children's librarian in Minneapolis Public Schools. In 2013 and again in 2015, she won Minnesota State Arts Board Artist Initiative grants for her writing. She loves dogs and has a chocolate Labrador retriever.